What Would a Guinea Pig Do?

Kate Duke

E. P. DUTTON   NEW YORK

Published in the United States by E. P. Dutton,
2 Park Avenue, New York, N.Y. 10016,
a division of NAL Penguin Inc.

Published simultaneously in Canada by
Fitzhenry & Whiteside Limited, Toronto

Designer: Barbara Powderly

Printed in Hong Kong by South China Printing Co.
First Edition   W   10 9 8 7 6 5 4 3 2 1

Library of Congress Cataloging-in-Publication Data
Duke, Kate.
  What would a guinea pig do?/Kate Duke.—1st ed.
    p. cm.
  Summary: Includes three brief tales about what
a guinea pig would do in different situations.
   ISBN 0-525-44378-9
  [1. Guinea pigs—Fiction.] I. Title.
PZ7.D886Wh 1988   87-22175
[E]—dc19   CIP
                                   AC

What if a guinea pig wanted to clean up his house? What would he do?

He might decide to wash it out.

But that wouldn't work very well.

Maybe he'd get someone to do it for him.

But that would be a big mistake.

He might get a vacuum cleaner....

But that would make things go
from bad to worse.

Thank goodness for a friend!

Now what would that guinea pig do next?

Have a party to celebrate—

and start all over again!

What if some guinea pigs wanted to bake a cake? What would they do?

They'd get out their baking tools

and look around for a mixing bowl.

Then they'd get some flour

and butter and eggs,

and sugar to make the cake sweet.

They'd put all those things in the bowl—

plus a few extras,

and mix them up.

Then they'd wait while it bakes.

But what if, after all that hard work, the cake looked like THIS?

Then what would those guinea pigs do?

Eat it!

What if a guinea pig wanted
to be like somebody else?
What would she do?

She could try some stripes

or curl her hair

or add a few feathers.

She could make herself taller

or faster

or louder—

oh no!

Now what would that guinea pig try next?

Maybe she'd decide that best of all
she likes being a...

guinea pig!